# THE BALLAD OF THE SHIRLEY T AND OTHER STORIES

# THE BALLAD OF THE SHIRLEY T AND OTHER STORIES

BY

PERRIN COTHRAN CONRAD

iUniverse, Inc.
Bloomington

**The Ballad of the Shirley T and Other Stories**



*This is a work of fiction. All of the characters, names, incidents, organizations, and dialogue in this novel are either the products of the author's imagination or are used fictitiously.*

*iUniverse books may be ordered through booksellers or by contacting:*

*iUniverse*
*1663 Liberty Drive*
*Bloomington, IN 47403*
*www.iuniverse.com*
*1-800-Authors (1-800-288-4677)*



*ISBN: 978-1-4620-5671-2 (sc)*
*ISBN: 978-1-4620-5672-9 (ebk)*

*Library of Congress Control Number: 2011917191*

*Printed in the United States of America*

*iUniverse rev. date: 10/14/2011*

# Dedication

This book is dedicated to the memory of Dr. Bo Ball, who was my Creative Writing professor at Agnes Scott College.

# Contents

# The Ballad of the *Shirley T*

The forecast called for a hot July day, but it was only 4 a.m. when Henry Lee Geathers stepped down out of his trailer. He tried not to wake his wife, Daisy. But today, like always, she stirred slowly and got up to make Henry a pot of coffee. When he thanked her, she just said it was the least she could do. She tried to stay busy since she'd been let go from her job in the seafood store. She was a hard worker, but they couldn't afford to keep her on. The new Wal-Mart fifteen miles down the highway had a fancy lobster tank, and hardly anyone ever came into Billy's Seafood anymore.

Henry heaved himself over the side of his shrimp boat onto the deck. Alfred, his striker, would be along shortly. Tide was low, and a gentle zephyr blew at about ten knots. Henry thought he heard a gator slink through the crackly marsh grass on the other bank and scratched his chin. Once the color of a milky chocolate bar, his skin now matched the dry ash of the oyster pit in his front yard. He heard Alfred's quick footsteps on the dock.

"'Bout time, you old fool," Henry said as Alfred clomped into the boat in his white rubber boots.

"Who you callin' a fool? You the one got people after you." Diesel fumes rolled over the dark river, and they shoved off.

They were in the Intercoastal Waterway before Henry asked, "Who's been after me?"

"White man by the name of Ravenel came looking for you yesterday. Said he was from town." Alfred cocked his chin sideways and rubbed behind his ear with a bony index finger. When Henry didn't fill the pause, Alfred continued, "Said he was from the IRS and nobody was at home to your house."

Henry cleared his throat. "You know my little grand, Clarice, got bit by a rabid coon."

"Mm-hm." Alfred nodded slowly.

"Daisy and me went to town to see her in the hospital yesterday. My grand might not live to see the next daybreak, and that man won't let up."

"He don't care about your grand. He wants your money."

"I know that's right. Clarice and her mama don't have insurance, and they need my help."

"Mm-hm." Both men nodded in the early morning light and understood what was not said: the government might take Henry's boat. Henry's father had built the boat with his own hands almost sixty years earlier and called it *Shirley T* after Henry's mother. Henry wrinkled his brow and swallowed hard at the thought of losing it. He swallowed again harder at the thought of losing Clarice, and all because he wasn't watching her when the coon attacked her. She was only four and lived in the city. She didn't know to be afraid of a "big cat with a mask," as she had said afterward.

"Daddy, forgive me. I don't think I can save either one of them," Henry moaned after Alfred had gone out onto the deck to guide the nets and doors over the side. Henry's chest was heavy with grief.

When the *Shirley T* whirled up to the dock at the end of the day, a man in a light gray suit was there waiting.

"Good afternoon, Mr. Geathers!" he called as Alfred and Henry tied up the bow. Remember me, sir? I'm Bill Ravenel. I've been out to see you before regarding your shrimp boat. Could I have a word with you?"

Expressionless, Henry walked down the port side and shook Ravenel's hand. Folding his arms, he said, "I hear you been looking for me."

"Yes sir, you're a hard man to find. Tell you what . . . why don't we go sit in my car over there so we can talk privately."

"Here's fine." Henry didn't move.

Ravenel wiped his forehead with a handkerchief. "I could give you a lift home and we could chat on the way."

Henry smirked. "I live a hundred yards from here."

Ravenel sighed and frowned a little. "That's right, isn't it? Okay, Mr. Geathers. If you want to do business that way, then we'll quit beating around the bush. You owe the Internal Revenue Service $6,000.00."

"$6,000.00?" Henry frowned at a number larger than the one he remembered.

"Yes, with the added interest, it comes to a little over $6,000.00. Would you happen to have that sum today?"

"Not today." Henry half-chuckled, knowing he didn't have it on any other day, either.

"Well, I'm afraid you have fourteen days to come up with it. We've already had a lien on your boat for over six months. If I don't see that money, you know we'll have to take possession of the *Shirley T*." Henry stared down at a stray mullet flapping around on the deck.

"My granddaughter is sick in the hospital."

"I'm very sorry to hear that, Mr. Geathers. Hope she's better soon. I'll expect to see you in the next fourteen days. You have my number. You know where to reach me." Dust billowed behind Ravenel's white Dodge.

Henry wended his way up to the trailer and went inside to the smell of collards on the stove. Daisy was there in a flowered house coat. "They cut off our phone today, Henry. I went up to the store to call Gladdy, and it's not good. Clarice got real bad last night. Her fever went up. She's unconscious." She flopped down on the orange corduroy couch next to Henry, and caught a familiar whiff of his fishy-smelling sleeve.

"She gonna come out of it?" Henry was quiet. He almost whispered.

Daisy sniffed, "Gladdy don't think so." The two stared out the front window at the evening sky; fuchsia, pink, coral and orange fell into the horizon over the marsh. Daisy got up and stepped toward the bedroom. "I'm gettin' dressed and goin' over to the hospital after we eat."

"I can't go."

"'Cause it was your fault? You're a sorry somethin', Henry." Henry thought she was right and rose to clean himself up for the trip to town.

When Daisy and Henry finally pulled back into the driveway and got out of the truck, it was 4 a.m. They stumbled up the front steps. Alfred came jogging up the path from the dock.

"Henry! Where you been, old man? Are we goin' out today?" Henry motioned Alfred inside.

Once inside, Daisy shuffled silently to the bedroom with a handkerchief covering part of her wet face. Henry sat down in the chair closest to the door. "She's gone, Alfred. She passed a couple of hours ago. I can't go today. Just can't. Sorry."

"Oh, yeah . . . hey, it's all right, man. Sorry. Sorry about Clarice."

"Alfred, Gladdy owes the hospital over $22,000.00." Henry leaned forward to put his head in his hands.

"She don't have Medicaid?"

"No, no. She just missed qualifyin'. Makes too much at her job. She asked if I could help. What could I say? She's my baby. But I don't got it. I'm in deep. Don't got what I need, much less what she needs. I reckon she'll be needin' help with a funeral, too."

"Yeah." They sat in the dark for several quiet minutes. Alfred stood and put his hand on Henry's shoulder. "Let me know if there's anything I can do." Then Alfred slipped out the front door.

Just after sun-up, Henry loitered in the front yard, nursing a cup of coffee. He lazily kicked a rock at an old cur sniffing around Daisy's flower bed. Daisy wrestled a suitcase down out of the trailer.

"Whatcha doin', woman?"

"Gladdy needs me, Henry."

"I might need you, too."

"You can feed yourself. It's only temporary. I'm gonna find a job in town and help her pay off Clarice's medical bills. She needs company, too. She'll be lonely."

"My foot. That girl ain't never been lonely a day in her life. She got enough men friends . . ."

"I ain't listenin'. If you so worried, you come, too."

"No, I gotta figure a way to hold onto my boat."

Daisy got into the truck. "You come tomorrow, and bring your suit for the funeral." With that, she wheeled away.

Henry walked up the road and knocked on Alfred's door. Alfred opened it and stood puzzled in his underwear. His skinny arms held out a bowl of shrimp and grits. "You wanna come in?" His white beard was glowing in the dim sunrise.

"Daisy just left. Ain't no point in hangin' around here. Let's take off."

"Oh. Well, let me get dressed." Alfred disappeared into his dark little house.

"I'll go home and get my boots." Henry climbed back into his trailer and poured another cup of coffee. He yanked on his boots and ran out the front door. He wanted to get far away from the place where his negligence had killed his granddaughter.

When Henry and Alfred approached the dock later that day, thick, black smoke puffed up from the trees. The boat had barely bumped the dock when Henry leapt and hit the ground running. "Tie up, Alfred!"

"Be careful, man!"

Henry heaved and puffed down the path to an infernal heap of garbage. It was all gone. Flames licked the trees around what used to be the trailer, and sheets of ash rose with the heat of the chemically-charged fire. Henry stood in disbelief until Alfred came up behind him.

"You got insurance on it, right?" Henry didn't answer. "Henry, you can stay with me." Henry still didn't answer.

"All I got is the *Shirley T*, and they're gonna take it." Then Henry's mouth hung open a minute and he knew how the fire had started. "The coffee. I didn't turn that damn pot off." Henry turned and walked briskly toward the boat.

"Henry! Fool, ain't you gonna call the fire department?" Henry didn't slow his stride.

"What for? It's gone, and it's my fault." Henry jumped over the side and went into the cabin of the *Shirley T*. Alfred ran down onto the dock after him.

"What you doin'? What's got into you?" Henry revved the engine.

"Gimme a shove off."

"*Where* are you goin'?" Henry turned around to face his striker.

"Where they can't take my Daddy's boat. Goodbye, Alfred."

The two men nodded solemnly to one another, and Alfred pushed the stern away from the dock. *Shirley T* hummed out to sea with a gentle spray behind her.

# Gold Diggers

Vivian's footfall was quick and happy as though she walked in rhythm with some popular dance tune from the radio. Gold silken waves bounced behind her snappy stride across Morris and Epstein's thin grey carpet. There was to be a new employee moving in next to her today, and she had worn her red suit in hopes that it would be a man. But when she reached her desk, cluttered with plants and photos in expensive gold frames, the neighboring cubicle was empty.

"Good morning, Margaret!" she called out to a grey-haired woman across from her.

"Good day, Vivian." Margaret did not look up from her computer.

"Have you seen the new guy yet? Isn't he supposed to be here today?"

"The new 'guy' is a young woman, and no, she isn't here yet."

"Oh. Well, how does she think she can be late on her first day?"

"She can do whatever she likes, because she is Mr. Epstein's granddaughter. Her name is June, and I suggest we all be nice to her, lest she should make disparaging comments about us to Mr. Epstein."

"Oh." Vivian sat down and flipped the power switch for the equipment on her desk. She put her hand on her chin and again said, "Oh."

"What?" asked Margaret with a sigh.

"She could prove to be quite a useful ally, eh, Margaret?"

For the first time, Margaret's eyes lifted from her screen. "I hope she proves to be a pleasant co-worker, Vivian." Margaret had barely completed her sentence when Mr. Epstein's secretary, Betty, rounded the corner with a red-haired girl in her early twenties. As they came closer, Vivian's smile faded in response to the sour expression staring back at her.

"Good morning, ladies," Betty began. "This is June Epstein. She will be working with you all from now on. June, this is your cubicle."

Vivian stood up. "Hi, June! I'm Vivian! How do you do?"

"I do fine," June said in monotone.

Before leaving, Betty added, "If you have any questions, just ask Vivian or Margaret . . . Good luck!" June sat down and began rifling through her drawers and cabinets. She pulled only a desk calendar out of her bag. Vivian guessed this was her idea of decoration for her area.

Vivian tried making conversation, but June barely looked at her. "So June, where did you go to school?"

"State."

"Oh, really! My brother went to State. Maybe you knew him. What year did you graduate?"

"Didn't."

"I see. So, um . . . where do you live?"

June looked at her as though she had just asked what color underwear she was wearing. "Downtown."

"How nice! So you're close to the office." With this, Vivian decided to go back to work and try again later.

After lunch, she came back with a gift-wrapped package which she presented to June. "It's nothing big, June, but it's my way of saying 'welcome.'"

June turned the gift over in her hands for about ten seconds. She screwed up her face and said, "This is very interesting wrapping paper." Finally she tore one end and pulled out a white box with a gold frame just like one of Vivian's. "Oh, a picture frame."

"Yes! I thought you might want to keep a photo of your family on your desk or something." She waited anxiously for June's response.

June simply said, "Okay."

The next day, Tuesday, June scowled through her red bangs at the cursor on her terminal. "How does it expect me to type the password when I don't know it?" She pulled a thick, blue manual out of her top drawer and dropped it on her desk with a vibrating boom. "I don't even know how to look it up in this stupid book, and I don't care, either. I don't even want to be here. It smells like gym class in here."

Vivian, who had been trying to ignore June, rolled her eyes and said, "It should be in the Table of Contents under 'Setting Passwords.'"

"Why do they have passwords to get into programs you need to access all the time, anyway? I think it stinks."

"Well, you know, June, they have to keep undesirable people from getting to company information. Otherwise, any incompetent wretch would be able to get to our files. It had you stumped, didn't it?"

June stared down at Vivian's too-short skirt, spray-tanned legs and Prada heels. Then, she very thoughtfully said, "That's a stylish skirt you're wearing, Vivian."

Vivian smiled. "Why, thank you, June."

"Did you shrink it in the wash, though?" June smiled for the first time. "I'm glad my grandfather owns the company and I'm assured an eventual promotion. I don't have to flirt my way to the top."

Vivian set her jaw and tossed her head to the other side. "I think I'll take my coffee break now." She shot away—a blonde bullet.

Wednesday arrived, and Margaret, June and Vivian sat at the round table in the kitchen during lunch hour. "The vice-president is coming tomorrow," Margaret warned.

"What vice-president?" June yawned.

"Kennedy Bauer," Vivian beamed. "Of course, I already knew he was coming in town. He called me last night, and we made plans for tomorrow night."

"Oh yes, I forgot you two had an . . . 'affinity.'" Margaret said disgustedly.

"Why is Kenneth Brower so important? Why should we have to be ready for him?" June asked.

"Bauer. Bau-er. Ken-ned-y Bau-er." Vivian leaned across the table and enunciated carefully to make sure June got it, but June stared at her blankly. "And the reason he's important is that when Mr. Epstein retires, Kennedy will probably take his place as president of the company."

"I don't know about that, Vivian," Margaret said. "I believe Mr. Tanner will get that promotion before Mr. Bauer, since he's been here about twenty years longer, among other things." She stopped and laughed. "Unless, of course, Mr. Bauer marries into the family or something!"

Vivian tittered nervously. "Well, I have a clothing predicament, and maybe you ladies can help me. Tomorrow night, we're going to a barbeque at someone's house. That will be casual, of course. But then he's taking me to see that new play at the Hanbury Theatre, and it's opening night. Now, my problem is obvious!" She paused for dramatic effect, knowing very well that they failed to see or understand her problem. She expounded. "The barbeque would be a skirt and sweater affair at most, or maybe even a nice slacks kind of function. But the opening night of a play demands a cocktail dress, at the least. I certainly can't wear a cocktail dress to a barbeque at someone's home! I'd feel like a fool! What should I do?"

Margaret and June continued with their apathetic stares. "I think it's time for me to go back to work," Margaret said.

June got up to follow Margaret and replied, "Maybe if you go naked, you can capture your vice-president much quicker and more efficiently."

Vivian thrust icy daggers through June. "June, I have tried to be nice to you. I don't know what you could possibly have against me, because you hardly know me. Now, you've made several comments to the effect that I am fast and loose, and I would like to know where you're getting this."

"My grandfather." She smiled and left Vivian alone in the kitchen. It was true. Vivian couldn't deny the number of higher-ups in the company with whom she had flirted, but she didn't think Mr. Epstein knew it. She didn't know how to touch-type and she had majored in Art in college. The only reason she made it all the way to sales agent status was because she'd had an affair with the manager of the department. But she worked hard to stay there. And she was hoping to get promoted to sales manager in the next year. She was no dummy, and she had put in overtime hours for the department. What was wrong with giving yourself a little boost?

Suddenly at 11:30 the next morning, Kennedy appeared like a specter before her desk. It gave her a start, but she smiled coyly and tossed her hair. He rested his hand on the edge of her desk, and leaned in so that his Gucci cologne wafted toward her.

Vivian took a deep breath. Almost in a whisper, she said, "Hello, Kennedy."

At the same volume, he replied, "I'm going to lunch with Mr. Epstein. Would you care to join us, Darling?"

Her eyes grew desperately wide, then she furrowed her brow. "I have a lunch meeting . . . but I could postpone it!"

He stood up straight again and said, "Oh no, I wouldn't want you to push a client aside. Who is that young woman standing at the copy machine?"

"Oh, her? The one at the copy machine?"

"That's what I said. Yes, the red-head."

Vivian bit her bottom lip. "That's June Epstein."

"I thought it must be. I'll introduce myself." Kennedy sauntered over and talked to June, who wrinkled her nose and had a look on her face like a fly was buzzing around her. Vivian couldn't hear the conversation, but now Kennedy was carrying June's copies back to her desk. As soon as they were back within earshot, Vivian pounded away on her keyboard and looked very busy.

"I think your grandfather would be very pleased if you joined us for lunch, June. I know I'd be pleased." He stood in front of her desk with his hands in his pockets.

June smirked. "Wouldn't you rather take Vivian? She's your girlfriend or something, isn't she?"

"Oh, no! Well, you know . . ." He glanced nervously at Vivian, who was fondling her letter opener, with venom in her stare. "I mean, I'd just like to welcome you on board, June. What do you say? We're going to the Fox and Hounds."

"So does a vice-president always take new employees out to lunch?" June asked skeptically.

Vivian could retain her ladylike manner no longer. "No, just the pitiful ones who were only hired because of family connections. He's just brown-nosing with the boss, June."

Kennedy leaned across June's desk and pleaded, "Don't listen to her, June. Some people don't know how to be professional and polite when they feel threatened. Mr. Epstein doesn't even know that I'm asking you, and we'll only be an hour."

"Well, okay. Let me get my purse."

At 1:30, Vivian had already been to her lunch meeting and returned. She tapped her toe on her plastic mat and wondered how June thought she could stay away at lunch this long, granddaughter or not. Just as she was about to report her to the manager, Kennedy came around the corner alone and walked up to her desk. He had a sheepish grin on his face.

"Vivian, I hope you can forgive me, but I'll have to break our date for tonight. Something's, uh, come up. I told Mr. Epstein I'd take June out, you know, to tell her more about the company. I promise I'll make it up to you. Rain check?" Vivian glared silently. "Well, Sweetheart, it will *have* to be okay, because it's important for my relationship with Mr. Epstein that I do this. This could really make a difference in my future with the company."

Very sedately, she asked, "Are you going to take her to the barbeque and the theatre?"

"I hadn't thought about it. I do already have the tickets reserved for the play, although I haven't picked them up yet."

"What about the barbeque?"

"I told them I would be coming with a date. It would be rude not to show up. Well, I hope all is understood." An awkward silence hung between them. Vivian could hear Kennedy breathing hard through his nose. He only did that when he was lying, or when he was telling her something he knew she didn't want to hear. "By the way, do you still have my credit card? I remember letting you use it before, but I don't think I ever got it back."

Vivian thought of the card in her purse. "Yes, it's at home. I'd forgotten all about it. I'll get it to you through the mail or something."

"Brilliant. Well, I have to run now, Darling." He gave her a cursory peck on the cheek. "I'll call you sometime!"

Vivian watched until he was safely around the corner. She then flipped through the phone book until she found Hanbury Theatre. She dialed the number. "Hello, is this the ticket office? Yes, I'd like to cancel some ticket reservations for tonight . . . The name is Kennedy Bauer . . . B-A-U-E-R . . . Yes, that's for tonight's show . . . Thank you!"

A devilish grin spread across Vivian's face. Margaret, who had been fairly quiet all morning, inquired as to Vivian's seemingly unnatural happiness. "What are you doing over there, Vivian? It must not be work."

"Oh, but it is, Margaret. It's dirty work, but it has to be done." Vivian didn't care anymore that June was still with her grandfather, taking a long lunch. She didn't care that Kennedy had designs on June just because she was the boss' granddaughter. She had sabotaged their evening. And now she noticed there was something else she could sabotage. June had left her computer on inside the program she'd been working on all day. Vivian made sure June wasn't coming. With the stroke of a few keys, she erased all of June's work for the day. Margaret shook her head and peered through her pink-framed bifocals.

"Vivian. What do you think you're doing?"

"Protecting my best interests, Margaret. Practical and romantic. I'll kill that wench before I let her have my man or my promotion."

Margaret took off her glasses and said, "You're behaving irrationally. Why don't you take the rest of the afternoon off and collect yourself?" Vivian thought of that American Express Platinum card in her purse. Kennedy had let her use it before their ski trip back in the winter.

She said, "Yes, Margaret. I guess you're right. I think I'll go shopping." Vivian went straight down to Saks Fifth Avenue and purchased a smashing taffeta dress. It was a great deal at just under four hundred dollars. She signed "Vivian Bauer" as he had given her permission to do before. She would just explain that she had bought it before he broke their date, thinking that he would surely want her to have something nice to wear to an opening night at the theatre. It was a final sale item, and could not be returned.

At home, Vivian dressed herself in a black trench coat, black sunglasses, black shirt, pants and shoes. She slicked her hair back into a bun and looked for a hat. All she could find was a sun visor with the name of her parents' country club on it, but it served the purpose. Kennedy didn't know her country club, and it covered the top half of her face. Just before she left, she looked up Kennedy's friends who were hosting the barbeque, and found their address. She grabbed a plastic squeeze jar of mustard and headed out the door.

When she found the house, she parked two houses down, and on the other side of the road. She leaned the seat back a bit so it looked like no one was in her car. Kennedy and June arrived shortly after. June was wearing the same tight sweater and slacks she had on at work. Vivian watched them go in. She got out and slunk down the street to Kennedy's red Porsche. *Red paint fades very quickly*, she thought as she whipped out the mustard and sprayed it all over his beloved vehicle. She took care to douse the door handles with extra mustard.

As soon as the gold goosh covered the car, she ran back to her own Volkswagen and drove to the theatre to wait for them. All the way there, she squealed and giggled at the thought of Kennedy's face when he saw his car. He would want to go to a car wash right away. At this time of night, he would have to go to one of those gas station car washes, something he said he would never do. Even if he and June never showed up to the theatre, she was happy with what she had done. She smiled to herself as she slid around the outside of the ticket office, unnoticed.

Just before 8:00, the couple rounded the corner from the parking garage. Mustard stains all over the front of June's pants and Kennedy's rolled-up sleeves shone in the dim light of the street lanterns. It was obvious they had tried to clean themselves up, but had only smeared the condiment all over. This sort of thing didn't usually bother men as much, but for a *woman* to go to the theatre looking like that? *What's wrong with that girl?* Vivian wondered. She could see a weariness on Kennedy's face, and she reveled in how his night was only going to get worse.

As they walked into the theatre, Vivian stood behind the door in a crowd of people waiting to get in. Vivian followed them inside the door and ducked behind a large, potted Ficus. Kennedy approached the Will

Call window. Vivian could not hear very well, but she could see his face. It went from annoyed to angry. June glanced around the lobby, seemingly unaffected. Kennedy stepped back and explained to June that the tickets had somehow been erroneously cancelled, then re-sold to another patron. It was a full house, and there was no chance that they would see the show.

After a short exchange, June and Kennedy decided to go next door and get coffee. The lobby was starting to clear out, as the show was about to start. June went to the Ladies Room, and Kennedy waited in the alcove outside the bathrooms. He lingered there, looking all around, as if to make sure no one was looking at him. Then he quickly jammed his index finger into his left nostril and wriggled it around for a few seconds before he brought it out.

Vivian stood against the wall with her mouth hanging open. *Gross,* she thought. She had never seen him do this before. Kennedy Bauer had picked his nose in public, and it was too much for Vivian to bear. She snickered. She giggled. Then she laughed right out loud. Kennedy immediately scanned the lobby, looking for the witness. He didn't see her, even after June emerged and they walked right past Vivian's Ficus to get out.

Back in her apartment, Vivian still laughed to herself quietly. *Kennedy is a gold digger in every way*, she thought. Then she laughed so hard that she had tears rolling down her cheeks. They deserved each other, June and Kennedy. Vivian went around her apartment, taking down pictures of him. The last one she came to was a shot of the two of them out on the slopes. She paused for a moment and decided to leave that one up, so that any visitors would know that she had been skiing in Colorado that year.

# Get Your Own

Galya Jenkins stood next to her mother in the Good Samaritan A.M.E. Church and stared at her grandmother's face in the metallic pink casket. Mourners wailed behind her as she reached out to touch the folded hands in front of her. It didn't look like Grandma. Her face looked plastic, but that wasn't the only part that bothered her. Galya whispered to her mother, "Why you ain't tell them that ain't how she do her hair?" Her mother, Loretta, just shushed her and dabbed her dry cheek with a tissue. The only person who fed Galya, made sure she had clean clothes, got her to the bus on time, was gone forever.

For as long as Galya could remember, she had lived with Grandma. Her mother hardly ever came home, and Galya would go weeks or months without seeing her. When she was there, Loretta only slept on the couch and fought with Grandma. There had even been a Christmas or two when Loretta had not shown up. But Grandma made sure Galya had everything she needed, and then some. Her bedroom was like a young girl's dream with its pink curtains and bedspread, doll collection, and stuffed animals. Grandma had even fashioned a canopy to match the curtains and hung it from the ceiling over Galya's bed. It reminded Galya of bright, pink clouds. Her bookcase and dresser were painted pink, too. Grandma went to parent-teacher conferences. She watched Galya do her homework. She knew her favorite foods. She made her clothes. She loved her. Galya knew that Grandma had protected her as long as she could from the truth about why Loretta never came home and what she did when she "worked nights."

In first grade, Galya got off the school bus thrilled one day. She ran down Azalea Drive and into the cinderblock house with its mint green paint peeling. "Grandma!" she called, "I know what Mama does at her night job!" Grandma dropped her mop and turned around. "She's a magician, right? Why you never told me that?!"

Grandma drew her head back and frowned. "Who told you she's a magician?"

"A girl in my class. Her mama says my mama does tricks. That means she's a magician, right?" Grandma just shook her head and told her that wasn't right.

"No, she ain't no magician, Baby. How 'bout a nice cup of hot chocolate?" She put her supple arms around her granddaughter and squeezed hard. The truth would come another day. And when it did, Galya realized that girl in first grade had meant to say that her mother *turned* tricks.

After the funeral, Galya sat alone in her bedroom. The house felt different now. Her cozy little room became a cavern full of shadows. Even the pink curtains and canopy hung like wash from a clothesline. The stuffed animals stared at her with blank, plastic eyes. She wanted to run away, but didn't know where to go. She felt smaller and smaller as the walls around her pushed out and cold air rushed in. Noises in the house echoed around her. Ladies from the church whispered in the hall.

"Mary did everything for that child," began one of them.

"I know that's right," added the other.

"She made some bad mistakes with her three kids, but she was sure tryin' to make up for it with Galya."

"Yeah. What's gonna happen to Galya now? She's only eleven. She can't be on her own all the time. And her mama won't look after her," added the other.

"Mm, mm, mm. Sister Hattie say she gonna look in on her from time to time."

"Hattie come over here this mornin' and made sure the child had somethin' to wear to the service. Said Loretta was still sleepin' when she got here." That was true. It was only an hour before the service when Sister Hattie knocked on the door. Without Sister Hattie, Galya might not have made it to the funeral at all.

"Mm-hm. Drunk, or on drugs, or both. But what gonna happen when Sister Hattie ain't lookin'?" The two women had no inkling Galya could hear their whispers, but the same questions haunted her. With one uncle dead from a drive-by shooting and another in jail for taking revenge, Loretta was all Galya had left.

She had asked Grandma many times to tell her about her father. But Grandma had only said Galya was better off without him. Galya didn't know his name, and had come to think over the years that maybe Grandma didn't know his name, either. Galya's grandfather had taken off and moved to New York long before Galya was born, when Loretta and her brothers were children. Galya asked her grandmother why she hadn't married again or gone looking for another man. Grandma had only laughed and said,

"Lord, child, what would I want with another one of them? They ain't nothin' but trouble."

True to her word, Sister Hattie looked in on Galya over the next few weeks. When Sister Hattie found her in the house alone at night, she would pack her up and take her home to spend the night. One night, Galya was thankful to hear Sister Hattie come in the front door. Thomas, who Loretta called her boyfriend, was smoking pot with some of his friends in the living room. Loretta was nowhere to be found. Galya was cowering in her bedroom with a bloody nose. All she had done to deserve it was to tell Thomas Grandma wouldn't have liked him smoking in her house. When Sister Hattie put her arm around Galya to take her home, Thomas yelled after them that Sister Hattie could have her. "Ain't nothin' but a ho, just like her mama!" he shouted. Sister Hattie called the police, but the house was empty by the time they got there. In spite of Galya's pleas, Sister Hattie called Social Services, but no case was ever opened. Thomas could not be found, and Loretta was good at talking her way out of trouble.

The landlord refused to transfer Grandma's lease to Loretta, so it wasn't long before Galya and her mother moved across town into an apartment. Sister Hattie lost touch with them, despite giving her phone number to Galya. Loretta snatched it from Galya's hand, tore it up and called Sister Hattie "one of them gossiping church bitches."

Galya felt like a fish that had been hooked and pulled up onto a dock. New apartment, new neighborhood, new school, new faces. The apartment she shared with her mother was dark like a cave, especially when her mother closed all the blinds. A big oak tree shaded their side of the building from the sun, but its branches also scratched the windows at night and made Galya pull the covers over her head. Her pink curtains had been left behind. She arranged her things in her room the best she could, and rearranged them, and rearranged them again. She couldn't make it feel like home. Some of Grandma's furniture had come with them, but it looked out of place in the apartment. A friend of Loretta's had borrowed a truck and helped her move things in. But wherever things were set down when they were unloaded from the truck was where they stayed. Loretta was gone all the time, and Galya was left with a mound of packed boxes. After a few weeks, Galya began pushing and pulling furniture around to where she thought it looked better. She unpacked boxes and put dishes away in the kitchen. If her mother noticed, she never said so. Loretta came in late at night, if at all. She was asleep when Galya got up for school in the morning and gone again when Galya got home.

Galya looked forward to her free lunch at school every day because she knew she would get something hot. She learned her way around and made acquaintances easily. But whenever the question, "Where you stay at?" required an answer more than "With my mama," Galya pulled away.

She took uneaten food from other kids' lunch trays after they finished. "You ain't gonna eat that apple? I'll take it!" Rolls, unopened milk, anything else she could stuff into her book bag. The other children called her the "garbage disposal," and said had the biggest appetite in the school. She just chuckled along with them. Sometimes, she would take things from the tops of garbage cans when she thought no one was looking. She did anything she could to make sure she would have something to eat at home.

At night, Galya had dreams about Grandma fixing her big breakfasts of eggs, grits and bacon. She dreamed about going to school with fruit and sandwiches in a lunchbox like she used to, and having warm cookies waiting for her when she got home from school. She could smell Grandma's collards, ham, and sweet potato pie. She felt warm and full and loved just for a moment in her sleep. But when her eyes opened, she was still skinny, alone and hungry. Sometimes when she got up, she would go to her closet and pull out some of Grandma's dresses and cardigans that she had smuggled from the house. Surrounding herself with the garments, she would bury her face deep in one of the cardigans and smell a trace of Grandma's perfume, Sweet Honesty.

Loretta would leave quarters for Galya to take her clothes to the laundry room next door to the apartment manager's office, but Galya was expected to do Loretta's laundry, too. Once every couple of weeks, Loretta would get her head straight and bring home some groceries. She would even remember that Twinkies were Galya's favorites, and pull them out of the bag with a big smile. Loretta would cook dinner, laugh and cut up with Galya and maybe even walk to the mall with her. For a few hours, she would act like an older sister, at least, if never like a mother. Galya clung to those days. But there were rarely two of them in a row, and Loretta would become snappish and sullen at any mention of Grandma. Then the groceries would be gone, and Galya was back to rummaging for other kids' leftovers at school. Once in the spring, Loretta was sober for a full week and applied for a janitorial job at the mall. When she found out she had failed the drug test and would not get the job, she went right back to staying out all night.

Galya never knew what nightfall would bring. She'd start to get a stomach ache around 4:00 in the afternoon for wondering. Loretta mostly stayed out until long after Galya was in bed. But when she was home in the evening, she usually had a gentleman friend with her. On those nights, Galya was sent to her room and told to stay there and lock the door.

There was the earthy, smoky smell that usually seeped into Galya's room when she was confined. She knew that was pot. But sometimes, there was a smell she had not identified yet. It was an acrid smell that gave her a headache. She always tried to stuff dirty clothes around the door to keep the smell out, but it still came in through the vent.

One night when Galya had locked herself in her room, she heard a familiar voice booming from the living room. She knew it was Thomas. Sliding into her closet to hide, she pulled the accordion door shut. She sat in the dark for almost an hour. Thomas and Loretta argued. They hollered. Furniture was knocked over and Loretta was screaming, "Put me down!" Galya heard a thumping sound that she knew was her mother's thin, frail body ramming the wall. When Thomas left, Galya waited for a while before crawling out of her room. When she did, she found her mother curled up on the floor, shaking and crying. She had a bloody lip and swelling around her left eye. Galya helped her mother up and brought bandages and ice from the kitchen. Loretta stumbled off to her bedroom and the incident was never mentioned after that.

A few weeks later, Galya sat near her door, doing her math homework. One of her mother's guests was visiting, and the voice she heard was that of a frequent visitor. He was a man who laughed a lot and even made her mother sound happy sometimes. Galya had taken a couple of sodas from school, and drank them around dinnertime before her mother came home. Now she thought she would explode. There were no two ways about it. She *had* to go. *Maybe they won't see me if I run fast,* she thought. She cracked the door open and waited until her mother and her guest had their backs turned in the kitchen. Galya darted into the bathroom on her tiptoes. *Yes*, she thought, *I made it! That ain't so hard!*

When she was ready to go back to her room, Galya opened the bathroom door and made a break for it. But now the man was sitting on the end of the sofa right in front of her. She gasped and dropped to the floor to crawl behind the end table, hoping he hadn't seen her. But he had.

Grabbing his 40 ounce can from the table, he shouted, "Hey, get your own!" Then he threw his head back and laughed. "Loretta, you didn't tell me you had a kid. That what you're hiding in that locked room? She trying to steal my beer!" He laughed again.

Loretta stalked across the room, pointing. "Get back in there!" Just as Galya slammed the door, she heard her mother say, "That ain't even my kid. But she got nowhere else to go, so I let her stay here." The words were a fist in Galya's gut. She sat down on her bed and rocked back and forth, hugging her knees. She prayed for God to take her to Heaven so she could be with Grandma again.

In the summer, there were no school lunches. But there were a few older ladies in the complex who would wave to Galya in the afternoons, and she offered to take their trash out to the dumpster for fifty cents. She was lucky to make five dollars in a week, but it was enough for her to buy a stash of peanut butter or cereal when the cabinets were empty.

On a hot June afternoon, everything in the apartment suddenly switched off. Television, lights, air conditioning all stopped. All the neighbors still had their power, and the manager told Galya that her mother had probably not paid the electric bill. There were plenty of candles in the house, though, so at least Galya could see after dark. But the temperature steadily rose and hit ninety-two degrees in the living room before night fell. Right after midnight, Loretta came in the front door. She flipped switches, cussed, and went back out. It was two sweltering days before the power came back on.

Galya's biggest problem was boredom. Days of sitting indoors and watching television made her feel sick and tired. She wanted to get out and walk. To the right of the apartment complex, there stood a dilapidated, abandoned house. Her mother had told her never to walk that way by herself. There were always men sitting on the steps of the house and drinking from brown paper bags. That house was between Galya and the mall, so she could only go the other direction toward a couple of gas stations, a Dollar Tree, and Hancock Fabrics. Beyond that, there were only office complexes and restaurants.

It wasn't long before Galya wandered into Hancock Fabrics. She stared up at a wall full of buttons and notions. Grandma had done some sewing, but Galya never paid much attention to it. Now she looked down at the threadbare shorts that Grandma had made for her two years before. They were getting uncomfortably tight, but she didn't have much left to wear in the summer. *Sure do wish I could sew,* thought Galya. *Then I could make clothes for myself and Mama, too.* She wondered if she could even make things to sell. Galya daydreamed about what she would do with the money.

Suddenly, a shrill voice across the store snapped her attention in the other direction. Galya looked between pastel bolts of cotton standing up on end. The smell of the dye was good, but it made her a little dizzy. A woman in her forties with a tight, dark brown bun on the back of her head was tossing fabric samples onto a table where some other ladies were looking at pattern books. The lady was shouting. "I can't *wait* three weeks for you to order this! With as much business as I do here, I would think you could do something to expedite the process. Call another store? Get the factory to overnight it?"

The employee standing in front of the tight bun lady was fumbling to pick up the samples. "I-I'm sorry, but that's the best I can do. It's on backorder. I know we have something similar in a Waverly over here." She gestured toward some fabrics hanging on the wall. "It has the same colors . . ." the employee trailed off.

"Oh, are you a decorator?" asked the tight bun lady.

"No . . ."

"Well, *I am*. Maybe you should let me do my job and stop trying to tell *me* what looks good," she boomed as she waved her hand around like a belly dancer. "These old *Waverly* prints are tired and passé," hissed the tight bun lady. Galya didn't know what Waverly was, but she figured it must be something pretty bad, the way the tight bun lady said it with her face scrunched. The tight bun lady didn't seem to care that everyone in the store was staring at her.

"Those are new for this season. We just got them in." retorted another employee standing nearby.

"Never mind," she said as she walked toward the work tables, still twirling and waving her hand. "I'll just go ahead and take what I've already got over here. I'm sure I can find what I want somewhere else. I don't know why I waste my time by coming here first." Galya wondered how many times that lady had yelled at people in restaurants and made them secretly spit in her food.

Galya turned back to a display of zippers in every color imaginable. She brushed her fingers across them and watched them swing back and forth. As she slowly moved to the next display, she saw spools of thread in even more colors. It was better than a rainbow. She pulled out one spool of her favorite pink, and drew a short breath when another spool sprang forward into its place. Then she didn't know how to get the spool back in, so she just set it down on a shelf. When she looked up, the tight bun lady was staring directly at her. Galya quickly looked away and shrank behind a display of velvet and tulle. The tight bun lady pointed in Galya's direction and raised her eyebrows. "You might want to watch that one," said the tight bun lady. "Potential shoplifter."

All she wanted to do was run out of the store, but Galya knew that would only make them think she really was shoplifting. She was frozen. A warm hand touched her back. *I'm going to jail,* she thought. *I didn't do nothing, but they're taking me to jail.* Her stomach felt like it was turned inside out. Tears were welling in her eyes when she turned around. The lady behind her had red hair, a round face, and a round, little body to match. Her eyes were smiling. Her voice was fresh and bright like a good cantaloupe.

"Do you need help, Sweetie?" The urge to clam up and run was overcome by instant, involuntary trust. Although the lady was white, there was something about her that was just like Grandma.

"No, Ma'am." Galya wanted to smile back, but was frozen with everyone looking at her. It was like she was the Washington Monument or something.

"Are you here with an adult?" The lady took Galya's hand and led her to the side of the store where tight bun lady could not see them.

"No, Ma'am." Galya figured she was still in trouble. They would kick her out of the store for being a kid without a grown-up.

The lady's smile faded. "Does someone know where you are, Darlin'?" Galya looked at her feet. She didn't want to tell this nice lady that no one knew, and no one cared. Worse yet, Galya was always afraid that someone would call Social Services to take her away and she would never see her mother again. If she waited long enough, she knew that her mother would come around. She knew they could have Twinkie days all the time. "Do you live close to here?" The lady persisted.

Galya felt safe enough answering that question. She pointed in the direction of the apartment and answered, "New Colony."

"What's your name?"

"Galya."

"Galya. That's a lovely name. I'm Ms. Sue. Do you sew?"

Galya looked up and smiled, "No, Ma'am, but my Grandma did, before she passed."

"Oh, I see. I'm sorry. Did she pass away recently?"

Galya thought for a minute. It seemed like a lifetime ago, but it was only seven months. "In the fall. I stay with my mama now, and she work during the day." She didn't mean to fib, but it just came out. And it sounded better than the way things really were, so Galya just left it like that.

"Well, we have classes sometimes if you'd like to learn how to sew." Galya just smiled and nodded. Ms. Sue patted her back. "Good. Is there anything I can help you with today?"

"No, Ma'am." Galya knew she was being politely booted from the store. She didn't mind it, though, coming from Ms. Sue.

"You come back and see me when you're ready to sew. And let me know if you need anything else in the meantime."

"Yes, Ma'am." Galya walked to the front of the store and looked back to wave at Ms. Sue.

Tight bun lady was at the cash register, writing a check. She looked up at Galya haughtily. "I didn't know you all had a problem with riffraff coming in here."

Ms. Sue straightened her back and said sternly, "We don't." Galya felt warm. It was like someone had been pulling down on her face and suddenly let go. Her cheeks felt weightless. Ms. Sue was sticking up for her.

Tight bun lady folded her checkbook and slipped it into the oversized bag on her shoulder. It looked like it was made out of giraffe skin. *Mean old lady probably killed that giraffe her own self,* thought Galya. Then she left the store with her head up.

One morning in June, Galya realized her mother had not come home for the last two nights. Different images flooded her head all day. One was of her mother sitting on a bunk bed in a jail cell. She knew Grandma had gone to bail her out once. Another image was of her mother lying dead in a ditch, covered with leaves and eyes wide open. Grandma had frequently yelled at Loretta that she would end up dead in a ditch. Yet another image was her mother lying in a bed in the ER. Grandma had gone there to pick her up a time or two. Every time one of the images would stay too long, she would shake her head like a wet dog. The "Gilligan's Island" marathon on television was her only distraction.

But the day wore on. And on. *What if she never comes back?* Galya wondered. How long would it take for someone to realize she was living there by herself? Where would she go? And how many of her things would she be able to take with her? She wished that she could call Sister Hattie, but she didn't know how. There was no phone, no phone book, no computer in the apartment. Tears came rarely anymore, but now she started to sob and curled herself into a ball in the recliner. All she wanted was for someone to tell her she would be okay. "Please, God," she cried, "please just give my Grandma back to me." Then the tears stopped.

Her heart felt a little lighter when she stood up. It was like a heavy box had been lifted off of her chest. She went into her mother's room to look around. She wasn't even sure why she went in there. But she thought maybe she would see a clue—anything—that would let her know her mother was okay.

The shades were drawn. There was only an unmade bed and a bedside table with a small television in the room. The rest of the room was empty, save a few boxes and a pile of clothes. She was afraid to flip on the light, but she tiptoed to the open closet. The empty hangers reminded her that Thomas had hit her with a hanger when she was very small, while her mother stood watching. She shuddered and ran her finger down her arm to the scar it had left. Grandma had banished Thomas from her house after that.

Then she saw it. It was sitting on the floor, shoved all the way to the back left side of the closet. She would know that tan plastic cover with the silver hinges anywhere. It was Grandma's sewing machine. Whether her mother had meant to bring it or not, it had made its way from Grandma's little rented house on Azalea Drive.

She lugged it into her bedroom and removed the cover. Her long brown fingers touched the presser foot, then traced the thread guide up to the top. There was still a spool of light pink thread sitting on top. Her fingers paused there as she realized Grandma was probably the last person to touch it. Galya went to her closet and found some light pink capri pants that Grandma had made for her the previous summer. She held them next to the sewing machine and compared. It was the same thread. She had almost forgotten she had these, and she tried them on now. They still fit just fine, maybe even better.

The sound of a key in the front door made her jump. She quickly covered the machine and pushed it into her closet, closing the door.

Loretta dragged some plastic grocery bags in the door, and set them down on the counter. "Galya?" Her voice cracked.

"Yes, Mama?" Galya stuck only her head out of her room.

"Help me put these groceries away, girl." She was still breathing hard from climbing the stairs to the second story apartment. She started to cough and flopped down into Grandma's burgundy recliner. There were frozen potato skins, Hungry Jack biscuits, orange juice, Coca-Cola, cookies, bread, Starburst, and a few cans of chili. Galya was starving and immediately put the potato skins into the microwave. When it beeped, Loretta rose from the chair and snatched the plate from Galya's hand. "Who said these were for you? Stay outta my food." Loretta ate the potato skins, then took the Starburst and Coke into her bedroom and turned on her little television. She slept the rest of the day and left again in the evening.

For several days in a row, Galya went to Hancock Fabrics looking for Ms. Sue. She was not there until the third day, but smiled when she saw Galya and asked if she were ready to sew. Galya nodded and told her how she had found Grandma's sewing machine. "That's wonderful!" Ms. Sue replied, as she finished off a bag of barbeque potato chips. Ms. Sue had crumbs on her cheek and blouse. Galya looked down at the schedule of classes that Ms. Sue handed to her. The next one wasn't for another three weeks.

Galya's shoulders sank. "Isn't there one before then?" The other employees were cutting fabric for customers and working the cash register. Galya thought the one with the red nametag and the half-glasses must be the manager. Ms. Sue held up a shiny, crumby finger toward her, gesturing she would be back in a minute. She gently steered Galya out to the sidewalk and looked her in the eyes.

"Are you really eager to learn to sew?" Galya looked at her blankly for a moment until Ms. Sue asked again, "Do you really, *really* want to learn to sew?"

Galya's eyes pleaded. "Yes, Ma'am. I do."

Ms. Sue nodded and took a pen and pad out of her apron pocket. She started to write. "I have a little alterations shop about a mile from here. I have it open part-time and work here part-time. Do you think you would be able to get a ride to this address? It's across the street from the Barnes & Noble." She handed the paper to Galya with greasy fingerprints on it. Galya's eyes darted back and forth as she thought of whether she could walk that far. It was closer to the apartment than it was to the fabric store. But it was also in the same direction as the mall, and she would have to walk past the abandoned house on the corner. *If I cross the street and walk on the other side, maybe that will be okay*, she thought.

"I can get there." Ms. Sue told her to be there Saturday morning at 9am. It was only two days away.

"Can you bring your machine with you?" Ms. Sue asked. Galya paused and thought about carrying that heavy machine for nearly a mile. She slowly nodded and bit her lip. "Okay," smiled Ms. Sue. "See you then."

On Saturday morning, Galya put on her pink capri pants, picked up Grandma's sewing machine, and started walking. She hobbled and bobbled with the machine bumping her in the leg every two steps. Before the bad corner, she crossed to the other side. She decided she would just cross back when she had to make a right, several blocks down. But as she passed the bad corner, she noticed a woman crying and hanging on a man's arm. The man was looking the other way. The woman was her mother. Galya froze and strained to hear across the traffic. Loretta was saying "please" over and over. Then she recognized the man as the one who had seen her running to her room in the apartment. He peeled Loretta off of his arm and walked away.

Galya quickly jogged away, down the sidewalk. The sewing machine banged against her leg faster and faster, scraping the sidewalk once or twice. She looked back only once. Loretta stood alone on the corner, looking up and down the road. She smoothed her skirt and put her hand on her hip.

But as soon as Galya saw Ms. Sue's shop, she forgot all about what she had seen at the corner. She looked down at the paper to make sure the address matched. 1900B Savannah Highway. This was it. It was a little brick house that had been turned into two commercial spaces. It had olive green shutters, trim and steps. A sign on the door said, "Sue's Alterations." Galya pulled the sewing machine up the steps and opened the door slowly, peeking in. There were two teenage white girls sitting up front at sewing machines. One had long, brown hair tied back with a big, blue ribbon. Galya thought she looked like a cheerleader. The other girl had short blonde hair and wore large pearl earrings. Galya didn't see Ms. Sue anywhere, and thought she must be in the wrong place. She started to back out of the door, but it creaked and the girls looked her way.

The blonde piped, "You must be Galya! Come in!" Both girls smiled warmly, but Galya still felt a little awkward.

Ms. Sue poked her head out of a doorway covered by a curtain, then hurried out to help Galya with the machine. She rolled up a bag of M&M's and stuffed them into her pocket as she bounced across the shop. "Hello, Dear! I'm so glad you made it!" She craned her neck looking back and forth at the small parking lot. "Did someone drop you off?" Galya just looked down and shrugged her shoulders. Perspiration covered her like morning dew on grass. "Did you *walk* here all by yourself?" Galya shrugged again and looked up. Ms. Sue's mouth was hanging open, and her eyes were wide with disbelief. "You walked a mile down that busy road carrying that machine? That won't do." Galya figured Ms. Sue was going to tell her she had to leave. She postured herself to carry the machine back out the door, but Ms. Sue reached past her and shut it. "In the future, if you need a ride, I'll come get you."

Ms. Sue showed her to a table beside the other two girls and helped her set up the machine. She introduced the girls as Molly and Ann-Marie. They were from Ms. Sue's church and were learning to sew, too. At the end of two hours, Galya held a pouch in her hand that she had made herself. It had a long, thin rope so it could be carried like a purse. She pictured Grandma standing in front of her, telling her how proud she was. Grandma had the widest smile in the world, and it had always shone like the noonday sun when Galya brought home artwork, a good grade, or a complimentary note from a teacher. *She would bust her buttons at me using her sewing machine*, thought Galya, and she sat a little taller in her seat.

Twice a week, for the rest of the summer, Ms. Sue would collect Galya at the entrance to the apartment complex and take her to the shop for sewing class, then take her home at the end of the day. Galya would help Ms. Sue around the shop sometimes, fetching this color thread or that size needle so that Ms. Sue didn't have to stop what she was doing and get up. Ms. Sue said what a wonderful help she was. She bought her lunch and gave her $5 for each day she was there. Only on Saturdays would Ann-Marie and Molly come for class. The rest of the days were just Galya and Ms. Sue, and that was how Galya liked it best. Ms. Sue asked a lot of questions, though, and it made Galya uncomfortable sometimes. Galya didn't mind talking about Grandma. But when it came to her mother or her home life, she gave the shortest answers possible and often just flat-out changed the subject.

On a hot July morning, Galya stood at the apartment complex entrance, waiting for Ms. Sue. The man who had seen her in the apartment was coming down the sidewalk. She tried to look away, but his gaze was fixed on her like a fly on honey. She stared down the street, looking for Ms. Sue's car. *Why she got to be late all the time?* Galya wondered. Ms. Sue was often late to pick Galya up, but Galya was always on the sidewalk on time. She didn't want Ms. Sue coming into the complex to look for her.

"You Loretta's girl, ain't ya?" Galya looked up at him, not knowing whether she should answer. But he smiled at her and chuckled, "Yeah, I know you." She couldn't help but smile back, because he seemed so nice. Then she remembered her mother hanging on him and begging, and she was embarrassed. "What you got there in that case?"

"Sewing machine," she answered.

"Your mama at home?" He gestured toward the apartment. She shook her head. "That figures," he continued. "So what you doin' with that machine? You know how to sew?"

"Yes," Galya said proudly. "And I'm gonna make things to sell, so I can make some money." She grinned.

"Well, look at you! That's good for you. But you know . . . you won't make much money sewing. How old are you?"

"Eleven." As soon as she said it, she knew it was wrong. She suddenly realized she had had a birthday a few weeks ago, but no one remembered. She had forgotten it herself. She was twelve now.

The man tilted his head. "Well, Baby, you're young yet, but I might be able to use you in my business. Are you interested in making some *real* money?"

"Doing what?" She looked at him sideways. She wasn't interested in doing anything like what her mother did.

"Carrying things to people. Making deliveries, kinda like a courier. You know what that is? It's easy." He handed her a card that said, *Jerry 555-7676*. "You call me when you're ready." Ms. Sue pulled up at the curb and waved.

"I have to go now. Bye."

The man grinned at her. "You call me when you're ready, Sweetheart."

Galya got into the car with Ms. Sue and they drove away. "Is that a friend of yours you were talking to?"

"Friend of my mama." Galya put the card in her pouch and wondered how much she could make working for him. Ms. Sue furrowed her brow and pursed her lips. Galya could tell Ms. Sue was getting ready to ask more questions. Galya headed her off. "What kinda snacks you got in your bag today?" There was always one salty thing and one sweet thing.

In mid-August, it was almost time to go back to school. Galya realized she would not be able to spend as much time with Ms. Sue when school started. She counted $48.00 and rolled it up. She put it back in the shoebox next to her box of food. She knew Loretta would eat anything she found, so Galya hid her food in the closet.

Galya scarfed down some potato chips and Easy Cheese, and then drifted off to sleep in Grandma's recliner. She didn't hear Loretta's keys jingling in the lock. Loretta shuffled over to the kitchen counter and began rifling through some mail. Finally she said, "You need to register for school." Galya was startled awake and the chips fell from her lap onto the floor. Loretta walked over and picked them up. "Where you get these? Did I buy these?" Galya just shrugged. "Now I *know* I didn't buy no Easy Cheese. I don't even like it. Where you get this stuff?" Then Galya realized she had been slack. She had left the box with the food in the middle of the floor without pushing it back. She got up and raced into her room to hide the box.

But Loretta followed her and saw it. "What is *this*? Peanut butter, crackers, bread, chips, cereal, where you get this stuff?!" Loretta was shouting now. "Why you hidin' this from me? Who give it to you?" Loretta grabbed Galya by the hair and got in her face. "Tell me! Who give this to you?"

Tears were welling in Galya's eyes. She didn't know whether it would be better or worse to tell her. "I bought it."

"With what?" Galya just set her jaw and didn't answer. Loretta slapped Galya's face. "I said with what?" When Galya didn't answer, Loretta slapped her again on the same cheek. It stung so bad it felt like the skin came off her face. Loretta still had her by the hair, and jerked her down to the floor. Galya yelped. "I put a roof over your head, and this is the thanks I get?!" Loretta released Galya's hair and began rifling through the closet. It didn't take her long to find the shoebox with the roll of fives and ones. She grabbed the money and held it up in her fist. "Well, looky *here*! What you been doin' to get *this* kinda cash?" Loretta flipped through the bills and counted them. Galya had never seen anybody count money that fast before. Loretta mouthed *forty-eight* and stuffed the cash in her pocket. "I'm asking you one last time. Where you get this?"

"I work a job." Galya had never seen her mother's eyes look like this before. They were slitty and red. Her face didn't even look right.

"What job?" Loretta spat a little as she spoke through clenched teeth.

"I help a lady in a sewing shop."

"Liar!" she screamed. "This is mine. You took this from me. You been stealin' from me since the day we come here." She picked up a pink lamp and threw it at Galya's head. Galya ducked, and the lamp crashed against the wall. Loretta shoved Galya down on top of the broken lamp. "Wait here! I'm goin' to see what else is missin'." She stomped into her own bedroom and ransacked it. As the sounds of slamming and tumbling boxes thumped through the wall, Galya knew she had to get out. Her face still stinging, she looked around the room at stuffed animals, clothes, books. *What do I take with me? God help me.* The answer came quickly and clearly. *The sewing machine.*

Galya picked up the machine and tore out the front door. She hurled herself down the stairs. She ran down the street toward Hancock Fabrics, knowing it was Ms. Sue's day to be there. Down the sidewalk, across the parking lot, she galloped. She looked back only a couple of times, but didn't see her mother. When she finally burst into the store with the sewing machine banging the glass door, she stopped running. She sat down on the floor to catch her breath. The manager came over to ask if she were okay.

"Ms. Sue here?" Tears still streamed down her cheeks.

"No, Honey. She had a death in her family, and she won't be back for a few days. What can I do for you?" The manager squatted down on the floor near Galya. She reached her hand out and put it tentatively on Galya's shoulder. "You're bleeding."

It was only then that Galya realized that the broken lamp had cut her leg. A gash about two inches long lay open on the back of her calf. Blood had run down to her foot and stained her tennis shoe. People in the store were peering over to see what was happening.

The manager helped Galya to a chair behind to the cash registers and told her to sit tight. Then she retrieved a first aid kit from the back of the store. "You just sit here a minute and catch your breath." The manager helped her clean up the cut and let Galya bandage it herself. Galya whispered her thanks. She thought about calling Jerry. What if he just took her back to her mother, though?

Galya saw a phone book on the counter and reached over to flip it open. She tried to find a listing for Sister Hattie, but there were too many Browns in the phone book. None of them seemed to be the right address or name. The manager asked, "Would you like to call someone?"

"No, Ma'am, I can't find her number." Then she thought of the church. They would know how to find Sister Hattie. "Wait, I'd like to try one more thing." She found the listing for Good Samaritan A.M.E. Church and called the number.

A young lady answered the phone, and Galya told her she was Mary Jenkins' granddaughter. "I'm sorry, but I'm new here," she told Galya, "and I don't know who that is. What can I do for you?"

Galya sighed, and her voice quivered. "I need to talk to Sister Hattie Brown. Can you give me her phone number?"

The girl stammered a moment and said, "I can't give that information on the phone. I could call her and ask her to call you back, though. What's your name?"

"Galya Jenkins. But I don't have no phone. She can't call me back. I was wondering if she could come pick me up."

"Hold on a minute." The girl dropped the phone down on her desk with a bang. Galya could hear her talking to someone in the background. She came back and asked, "I'm sorry, now what did you need? You need a ride?"

"I'm trying to find Sister Hattie Brown. I need her to come pick me up." Galya lowered her voice and continued, "I got nowhere to go."

"How old are you?"

"Elev-, uh, twelve. I'm twelve."

"What's your name?"

"Galya Jenkins." Galya was fast losing faith that her message was going to make it to Sister Hattie.

"And you're looking for a Sister Hattie? Is that right?"

"Yes. Hattie Brown. Hattie Brown. Sister Hattie Brown." Galya figured if she kept saying it, the lady would realize who Sister Hattie was.

"Hold on. I'll get the pastor." The church was not very big—only a few hundred people in all. *Maybe I called the wrong church*, she thought. Galya held the phone and waited about five minutes. People in the store were staring at her. She just wanted to leave. "Never mind," she said, and gently placed the phone back down. She thanked the manager and fibbed about having somewhere to go. *God, help me, please.* She wasn't even sure how to pray.

Galya hobbled a few blocks, switching the sewing machine to the other side so it wouldn't bang the sore leg with the cut. She saw a sign across the street. "Ashley Methodist Church." She stood there blinking for a minute. That was Ms. Sue's church. After a minute or so, she swerved through the halted rush hour traffic and into the church's parking lot. Why she was drawn to it, she could not exactly say. But if this church was anything like her grandmother's church, they would never turn away a stranger.

A dark blue Suburban wheeled in right behind her and pulled into a parking spot. Molly jumped out of the passenger side. "Galya? Is that you?" she shouted across the traffic noise.

Galya bumped her way over to the car.

"What are you doing here? Is that . . . your sewing machine?" Molly slid her purse out off the car seat and closed the door.

"Yeah," Galya forced a half-laugh, "Hey, you know when Ms. Sue coming back in town?"

"No, I didn't know she was gone. Do you need help with something?"

Galya took a deep breath. "I was tryin' to find a lady I know to give me a ride, but I couldn't get in touch with her. I thought Ms. Sue could help me, but she got a death in the family." Galya kept talking even though she knew what she was saying didn't make any sense to Molly. "If I could get back over to the north side, I could stay over there with somebody, but . . ."

Molly told her that she would go get the youth pastor. "We were just getting ready to have a youth council meeting. But I'm sure the youth pastor can help you. He's super-nice. I think you'll like him."

Molly motioned for Galya to follow, but she didn't. She had seen a black BMW pull into the parking lot. The window rolled down and Jerry revealed a bright, white-toothed smile. He was looking right at her.

"You still totin' that machine all over town?" He threw his head back and laughed the same way Galya had seen him do before. She made her way to his car. "What are you doin' here?" He gestured toward the church. Jerry's passenger had a gold tooth in front and was slumped down in his seat. It was tilted back so far, he was almost lying down. He was muttering into a cell phone.

She didn't know quite how to answer. "I was just lookin' for somebody."

"Well, I'm somebody," he said. "Come on and get in. I'll give you a ride."

"I ain't goin' back to my mama."

"Girl, I'm done with your mama." He shook his head. "She still owe me some money, but I'm lettin' it go. I ain't got nothin' to do with her no more." Galya put her hand on the back door handle. She smelled pot and drew her hand away. "What's the matter, Baby?"

Molly called out behind her, "Galya, I found him. Come on in!" Galya twisted her upper body around and looked at Molly. The youth pastor had come out and was standing on the sidewalk, too. Stocky and olive-skinned, he looked like he could be one of the youth himself. He waved at Galya.

"What you waitin' for?" Jerry asked. "You got a ride right here." He held up his hands. "I'll take you where you need to go." Galya looked down and saw the butt of a revolver sticking out of Jerry's pants.

Then she turned around. The sunset was starting to glow around the cross on top of the church. The shadow from it reached long across the parking lot toward her.

"Thanks anyway," she told Jerry as she walked toward the church, "but you don't know the way." She could hear Jerry shouting something about changing her mind, but she didn't think she would.

# Eat at Joe's

Marge switched off her alarm clock and rolled out of bed to the mirror. Squinting, she picked flakes of skin from the end of her nose with a poppy red pinky nail. She did not bother to wake her daughter, Lucille, because she knew Lucille would hear her through the paper thin travel trailer wall and get up anyway. Once, they had lived in a real house, before Lucille's daddy left.

Marge piled her hair high into its familiar beehive shape, donned her Pink Frost lipstick, Desert Sun blush, false eyelashes, and an orange polyester uniform with "Marge" embroidered on the breast. As she walked out the flimsy door, she bellowed, "Lucille! I'm goin'!" This was a final wake-up call to make sure Lucille made it to trade school on time. She was studying for a career in plumbing.

Marge waddled the two blocks to Joe's Restaurant at the 76 truck stop by the overpass, where she waited tables. The blue neon sign buzzed and flickered at her in the early morning light. She punched the clock inside the back screen door and started taking orders from tattooed men with "What fer ya, Darlin'?" and "Y'all doin' alright over here, Sugar?"

It was almost noon when he came in. About once a week, he appeared and Marge always knew him. He was always middle-aged, sometimes short, sometimes large, sometimes skinny. He usually drove a big rig. He came in different shapes, but Marge always knew him right off. She'd make casual conversation and convince him to try her special homemade apple pie.

This particular day, his name was Jake, and he had a beard. A burly man, Jake looked somewhat like her ex-husband Billy—like a logger. She told him so. He just nodded over his coffee. "I meant it as a compliment, Sugar." She grinned a silver-capped grin. She'd had gold fillings before Billy left her, but she'd had to melt them down for the money.

"Thanks, Ma'am. Could I have a refill on this here coffee?"

"Sure! And tell ya what—I'll get you a piece of my very own apple pie to go with it. On the house, of course!" She got up to go behind the counter.

"That's mighty kind of you, Ma'am."

She wished he wouldn't be so nice. It reminded her less of Billy. Maybe she wouldn't do this one after all. She glanced over at Jake. He was leaning up to scratch his rear. Nah—she'd go ahead. Billy used to scratch his rear like that. He was probably just like Billy! Now she could see it in his eyes. He'd left some helpless, tearful woman behind, with a child to take care of. Maybe he even left her for another man, just like Billy did. No, he deserved it. She was sure of it. She picked up a packet from her purse and went into the kitchen. She smiled sweetly at him.

With a big butcher knife, Marge cut him a manly logger portion of pie. She pulled open her pouch and sprinkled her sugared arsenic healthily on the pie. She thought of the poor soul he'd ditched, whoever and wherever she was. She carefully closed the pouch again and replaced it in her purse. Cheerfully, she waddled back out to the table and placed the plate in front of Jake.

"Eat up, Sweetie!" she said.

# When Mattie Stopped Crossing the Road

Mattie turned off Live 5 News and sat for a moment before pulling herself up from the faded floral sofa. The old wood boards beneath her feet creaked. Sheer curtains blew softly as she shut the window and removed herself from the roar of traffic outside.

Her husband Joseph had built the house for them with his own hands. He died two years after he finished it, when Mattie was not even 35 years old. She was left behind with three teenage daughters, Sherrise, Sherryl, and Shandra, who left home one by one over the months that followed. Sherryl and Shandra left home to chase after no-good men who never married them, and Sherrise moved in with a cousin downtown on Coming Street with dreams of "bein' somebody."

The little yellow frame house had stood there on Highway 17 for forty years, built in the day when few traveled that two-lane way. The same live oak tree had always shaded it from the north, with Spanish moss tickling the roof. Now the road was a wide, busy vessel, carrying residents of all the new subdivisions. There were people taking children to soccer practice, people going to dinner, people going to shop, people going to work, people going, going, going. It had been widened and widened again over the years so it was just a few feet from her front porch. Mattie wasn't sure where they all came from, or why they chose to come here. She just knew that she had always crossed the road to sit in her sweetgrass basket stand, and it used to be much, much easier. Development had its benefits, though. Now she could get $150, $250, or more for any of her larger baskets. But pulling her things across the road in a wagon used to be a simple task. Now she had to weave in and out of 4 lanes of cars waiting for the light, stand at the concrete median, then scurry across to the other side.

Sherrise kept in touch and lived in Atlanta. She called periodically to tell Mattie she needed to sell the house and move. "Mama, you'll get killed crossing that highway," she would say. "Crossing the road is all I know," she would tell her daughter. "Take that away, and I got nothin' left.

Mattie started to bed. "Ain't got a reason to stay up late no more," she said to no one. A skinny tabby cat scrambled out from under the sofa and flew under Mattie's feet. "Oh, Lord Jesus, help me!" she shouted as she went down hard and fast, and hit the wood floor with her 78-year-old hip. At a crack and the sound of the screen door slamming behind the cat, Mattie was out cold.

She woke in the emergency room at Roper Hospital. "Where am I?" she asked a nurse.

"Roper Emergency Room. Your nephew found you, Ma'am. He called 911 and they brought you here in an ambulance." Mattie tried to sit up but quickly howled and fell back onto the stretcher. "Oh, no, please don't try to get up. You most likely have a broken hip.

Mattie winced and said, "Who found me?"

"I'm not sure, but I think his name was Emmanuel. Tall young man. He said he was your nephew."

"Oh, thank God. Is he here? I got to tell him about that stray cat. Tripped me up."

"I'm not sure Ma'am. We're just waiting now for the ER doc to see you and get you admitted."

## SIX MONTHS LATER

Mattie sat at the window and waited for Emmanuel. When he finally pulled up in his GMC Envoy, Mattie got up and started collecting her baskets into the wagon on the porch. Pulling it one-handed with a cane was much slower than she wanted to be. Emmanuel helped her gather the baskets into the wagon and they crept to the side of Highway 17. The cars whizzed past in a blur. They waited, and waited. Finally a red light made a gap for them to get to the concrete island in the middle of the road. As they got across the three lanes of traffic going the other direction, Emmanuel steered the wagon to the little wooden lean-to with the hand painted sign, "Sweetgrass Baskets by Mattie Middleton." He helped his aunt hang a few of her best baskets on the front of the lean-to, and pulled the wagon underneath.

"Now, Auntie, will you be all right until I come back this afternoon?"

"Yes, child. Go on." She waved him away as she settled into her metal framed folding chair in the shade. Her hips were too broad for her skinny frame, but her baggy, brown dress gave her the appearance of a baking potato, big all over. Mattie looked down at the excess fabric spilling over the arms of the chair. The diesel exhaust from a dump truck billowed at them.

Emmanuel shook his head, "Are you sure about this? You can't move around too well."

"What else would I do? I been doin' this all my life. You think I ain't used to sittin' by the road? Now, go on!" Mattie picked up her bone and started working. Of all the tools she had used over the years to make her baskets, this was her favorite. The whittled end was sharp enough to stab someone.

Emmanuel threw his hands up. "You know what you're doing. I'll be back at two."

And that was how Mattie went on for a few months until the weather got colder. Emmanuel would take her across the road to her stand in the morning, then collect her at about 2 or 3 p.m. and get her back home. But when the colder weather came, it was harder for her move. Only on the warmest 70 degree days could she make the trip across the road.

On Good Friday morning, a light sweater was too much before it was even 9 a.m. The news anchors called it unseasonably warm. Emmanuel pulled into the yard behind the little frame house just in time to see the stray tabby dart across the yard. "Devil cat," he muttered. "If she wouldn't feed him, he wouldn't hang around." Mattie was not on the back porch waiting, so Emmanuel let himself into the screen door. "Auntie!" he called. Mattie appeared in her house coat on the opposite side of the kitchen.

"Joseph?" she whispered in a shaky voice. "Is that you?"

"Auntie, it's me. Emmanuel." He stood with one hand on the screen door. "Don't you want to go across the road today?"

Mattie stood in the doorway for a moment, then turned back toward the bedroom. "I don't think I'll go today."

Emmanuel stepped into the kitchen and said, "Auntie, are you feeling okay?"

"No, no, I ain't." Mattie shuffled over and sat down at her kitchen table, and Emmanuel settled into the chair across. Mattie rubbed her eyes and explained, "The Town wants to cut a road through here. *Condemn* my property. I have to move somewhere else." Mattie looked out the window, then back at Emmanuel. She pulled a folded letter out of her pocket and slid it across the table to him. "They'll tear down this house. This is the house that Joseph built for me." She glanced around the room. Tears brimmed and fell from her eyes. "It's like he's still here with me."

Emmanuel pondered over the letter for a few minutes. He said gently, "Auntie, you have about ninety days. What do you want to do?"

Mattie set her jaw and drew a wadded, disintegrating tissue from her pocket. She wiped the tears from her cheeks. "I want to stay in *my home* that my husband built for me."

Emmanuel looked around at the tattered curtains and sloping kitchen counter. The floor dipped and rose like a wave since a joist had crumbled from termite damage. The back door had a gap at the threshold big enough for any medium-sized vermin to fit through. And plenty had.

After a moment, he shook his head and said, "I heard they needed another entrance to Parker Point Plantation. I was hoping it wouldn't affect you, though. It's cheaper for them to buy you and a few others out instead of routing the road another way."

Parker Point Plantation was a new development that was big enough to be its own town. The main entrance was about a mile down the road. With over 10,000 homes, it had its own grocery store and shopping center. It had a golf course, four pools, eight tennis courts, and six miles of walking trails. Once an old rice plantation with a gorgeous maritime forest surrounding it, it had been leveled by bulldozers and littered with expensive homes, condominiums, and luxury SUV's belching fumes. There were many who had lived in the area all their lives and had fished in the surrounding creeks for their supper. They had gathered their sweetgrass there, and had passed down family property without deeds or wills. But too many of them had been pushed out in the name of progress.

Mattie had been fortunate, because she still had a place nearby to collect the sweetgrass. She still had her stand. Most were not that lucky. Some drove as far away as Florida to get their materials for the basket trade that had been passed from generation to generation. But now the "progress" had finally caught up to Emmanuel's Auntie. The letter said that she would be given fair market value for her property. *What's the fair market value of an old woman's spirit?* Emmanuel wondered.

His nostrils flared for a few moments, then he took his Aunt's hand in his. He said gently, "Auntie, you'll come live with me and my family until we figure it out. We'll find you a place you love. You'll see." He knew there was no sense in fighting the inevitable, so he meant to encourage her. He had seen too many friends and neighbors try to fight the same battle, only to lose. Those with the big bucks got what they wanted. Those without had no voice. "I know this is your home, but we'll find you a place you like even better. Just think of no stray cat, no mice and lizards getting in the back door, no sagging floors and counters . . ."

Mattie just looked at him blankly. "Lord, child, I can't move in with you. Your wife and family don't want no old woman in there mixing things up." She wagged her finger at him and smiled. "A cramp in your style. That's what old Auntie would be. And I don't wanna be nobody's problem."

"It's just temporary until we find you a place, Auntie. You'll see. Everything will be fine."

Three days later, Sherrise drove over from Atlanta in her Cadillac. Emmanuel was not surprised to see her looking more like Mattie each time he saw her. Her hips had gotten wider, and her cheeks had begun to sag slightly, just like Mattie's. She and Emmanuel presented Mattie with a choice. She could move to Atlanta and live in an "independent living" facility that was close to Sherrise's house, or she could go to a senior community on James Island, near Emmanuel and his family. The brochures were slick and colorful. Mattie told them that day trips on buses, water aerobics, and being served dinner in a fancy-looking dining room didn't feel right to her. "Don't think I'd be comfortable with that. I need to pray on this," she told them.

After a few weeks, Emmanuel found himself at Mattie's kitchen table again, listening to her announce her decision. Mattie picked up the phone and dialed Sherrise's number. "Baby, I want you to know it's nothin' personal. I just don't think I could live and die in Atlanta. That ain't me." Emmanuel knew his cousin would be relieved, just as he was, that a decision had been made. "James Island is far enough away from home, as it is," she explained to her daughter. But James Island it was going to be. Emmanuel arranged Mattie's move into her new apartment for the following month.

It was a Saturday morning when Emmanuel and his wife went in Mattie's back door to load her things into a U-Haul. "Auntie? Are you here?" They called out several times.

Emmanuel slowly pushed the bedroom door open. It creaked and fell back against the wall. An old suitcase was open on the floor. Piled in it with no particular order were old letters tied with string, a worn-out pair of slippers, a couple of pictures from family reunions, Mattie's Bible, and Joseph's faded hat that had been on the dresser collecting dust since the day he died. Some clothes had been pulled from drawers and tossed to the foot of the bed.

As Emmanuel's eyes scanned the colorful heap of fabrics, he suddenly noticed that his aunt was lying at the head of it. Eyes closed, bathrobe drawn tightly around her waist, she was still. Perfectly still. Curled into her right palm was a black and white photo of Mr. and Mrs. Joseph Middleton on their wedding day. Emmanuel walked over to touch her cold wrist. There was no pulse. He began to sob quietly, and his wife walked over to embrace him. "She got what she wanted," Emmanuel whispered. "She lived out her days in this house."

The road crew was from Boston. When the boss whistled, guys in hard hats jumped out of the cabs of bulldozers and backhoes. Others put down tools. They sat under the shade of an old oak tree dripping with moss, eating lunch.

"Shame this old tree has to come down," said one of the workers. His cheeks bulged with soggy sub sandwich. "Most of that trunk looks pretty hollow and rotten, though." He shrugged.

A second one reached into the sandy soil and picked up a long, smooth bone with a sharp, whittled end. "What's this?"

"I dunno," shrugged the first. "Trash. Just throw it in the back of the truck. Looks like you could kill a guy with that, though." They chuckled, and it was tossed into the back of a green dump truck headed for the landfill.

# Queen's Subject

Wanda scraped the last of the cherry crumble from the aluminum TV dinner plate and licked her lips. "Well, there's no more food," she hollered.

Terry Dean Trapbear, her common law husband of nearly eighteen years, yelled back from the shower, "If you didn't eat so much, we could probably afford another week in this joint." Wanda lay on the motel bed and stared at her bare feet, wondering whether the bedspread colors should be called teal and rose or turquoise and mauve. Her feet were cold, but the trouble of getting up to find socks was not worth disturbing what she called "apple bakin' time." She remembered the way she and Terry used to enjoy apple bakin' time together, just laughing at each other for hours, listening to music, cooking big portions of breakfast food, watching life speed right by them. Lately, she was alone in it. Terry only paced and grumbled when they smoked, telling her of his fear that someone would smell the earthy fumes. They had been evicted from the trailer park for missing rent too many times, and now found themselves in a motel with weekly rates. The sound from passing trucks on I-26 kept Terry up nights. Wanda slept fine, though.

The second time she heard the pounding on the door, Wanda peeled herself up and looked out the peephole. Terry stood in a towel with his eyes wide. "Well, who is it?"

"The manager," she said nonchalantly and flopped back onto the bed. Her dishwater hair flew into her face.

Terry stomped over to the door and opened it slightly. "Sorry, man, I was in the shower."

The manager craned his neck to see around Terry's head. "I've had calls again about the smell of weed coming from your room."

Terry laughed. It sounded forced. His freckled shoulders bounced beneath his wild, reddish-brown hair. "Man, I told ya, it ain't us. I don't know where that's comin' from."

"Look, I can smell it right now. I don't wanna have to call the cops on you, 'cause it looks bad on my motel, but I will. Any more reports and you're out." He pointed his finger through the crack in the door.

"Yeah, no sweat, no sweat. I promise, you smell anything, it won't be comin' from this room."

"And y'all owe me for this week's rent. Tuesday at midnight, or you're out."

"You got it. You have a good day now." Terry smiled and started to close the door, but the manager struck his palm flat against it.

"Hey. Don't forget. One more report, and you're out. *And* I call the cops." The manager's footsteps rang like bells down the metal stairs.

Terry closed the door quietly, chaining it. Wanda rolled over face down on the bed, wearing one of Terry's t-shirts and a pair of sweatpants that had been cut off to shorts. With no more food, a nap was all that was left to do.

"Did you hear that?" Terry barked.

A muffled "Mm-hm" was the best she could give.

"No more smokin' in the room. That's it. And we gotta come up with rent." Terry walked in circles. "You got any bright ideas where we can find the money?"

Wanda turned over onto her back and said, "Where are we gonna smoke, then? Ain't got no car."

Terry growled and grabbed a suitcase. He threw it down onto the bed next to Wanda. She flinched. "Get dressed, Wanda. I can't afford to get arrested again. I got no more passes. You understand?! I am *not* goin' to the big house."

At nine o'clock on Wednesday morning, the manager stomped back up the metal stairs to tell Terry and Wanda to pay up or get out. But when he knocked on their door, it pushed open. Unmade bed, food wrappers and beer cans on the floor, the smell of weed lingering in the curtains, but no Terry and Wanda, and no money left to pay for the previous week. He shook his head. "Lousy drug head crooks!" They had even taken the towels and the bedspread. "Good thing the TV was bolted to the wall," he mumbled.

Queen Trapbear cleaned houses for over 40 years, and she was good at it. She took her time, went into corners and crevices, moved furniture when she vacuumed, and made sure everything sparkled when she finished.

She held that her father was full Cherokee Indian, but her broad nose, full lips and cappuccino skin proclaimed her mother's African roots.

Her clients took good care of her, too. A Christmas bonus, a Thanksgiving turkey, school clothes for her two children, even a hand-me-down car. She had saved enough money over the years to buy herself a four room house in the country, a few miles outside the town limits. It was painted green and had a little porch on the front which she adorned with flower pots and a couple of lawn chairs. The day she found the lawn chairs, Queen had been helping one of her clients get her house ready for a shin-dig, then had gone to the husband's law office to clean it after hours. Her hands were cracked, shoulders sore, eyes bleary. But when she saw those old lawn chairs sitting on someone's trash heap, she perked up and pulled off the road. "They just need a little love," she said as she laid them in her trunk. She cleaned them up and repaired the plastic weave. Everything at her house might have been old, but it was clean and in good repair. She owed no man money.

Her rickety spine had demanded that she stop cleaning houses at age 68. But that didn't stop Queen from earning a living. "Idle hands are the devil's workshop," she would say. She returned to her old love of handiwork with the needle and thread. Queen sewed, knitted, smocked, and crocheted. Her loveliest works were her crocheted table linens and smocked children's clothes. One of her former clients had a children's clothing shop called Small Blessings on the town square, and pushed Queen's creations. They sold like hotcakes, and Queen never had an empty pocketbook. "The good Lord, He watches over me," she said.

Queen sat humming to herself and working on a tablecloth. She leaned forward when a taxi cab pulled up in front of the house. Terry and Wanda got out of the cab and unloaded suitcases from the trunk. Queen shook her head and got up to open the door. "No," she scowled, as they came up front steps.

"Momma, it's just for a few days, until one of us can find a job." Terry cocked his head to the side and looked about to cry.

"No!" She stood in the doorway with her arms folded.

"Come on, Momma! I got a good lead on a dishwashing job at the steakhouse."

"If that's the case, I'm gonna call and tell them you a no-good pothead. They need to know."

"You wouldn't do that to me." He stood at the top of the steps with his hands out to her. "Can I at least have twenty bucks to pay for the cab?" The driver stood next to his car expectantly. Queen knew she should go back inside and lock the door. But she took a deep breath and pulled a couple of wrinkled fives from her pocket.

"That's all I got. You'll have to come up with the rest on your own. You know you'll be sleepin' in my work room, so you better let my stuff alone and stay outta my way." Wanda opened her bags on the porch and collected enough ones to pay the cabbie. Queen shook her head and started back in to make up the pull-out sofa in her work room. *Just one night,* she told herself, but knew in her heart she wouldn't be able to turn her baby out.

"If you don't get 'em outta there, I will, Momma." Queen's daughter, Angel, owned a beauty shop in North Charleston. Angel had gone to beauty school at a young age, been smart with her money, and ran a successful business. She even had four other hairdressers and two nail techs working for her. "You know they probably got drugs in your house. You know that, right? Go look through their stuff right now, and I guarantee you'll find something. Weed, smack, something."

"I think it's different this time. They walked into town for a job interview today. Didn't even ask me for a ride."

"You *want* it to be different, but he's just gonna break your heart again. And I hope he don't break your bank while he's at it. Don't give them money, you hear me? Not one red cent, Momma. Not one."

Queen promised. After she hung up, she saw Terry and Wanda come walking back up the driveway. They had been gone the better part of the day, and now they were back, smiling and laughing. When they came in the door, they went straight to the kitchen. Wanda went into the cabinets and pulled out crackers, cans of chili, cereal. Terry had his head in the refrigerator, piling leftovers and sandwich makings in his arm.

Queen suddenly saw Terry as a five year old little boy standing in front of the refrigerator in their old apartment. His hair was still the same color and texture, and he had the same chubby hands. He was so sweet as a boy. It hadn't been until after high school when he got mixed up with Wanda that he had started doing drugs. Queen knew Wanda was trouble from the start. With her hair up in a side ponytail and her shorts too short, Wanda looked to Queen like a girl with a plan. It seemed for years like the only plan had been to bring her boy down. They hung out in smoky bars, rented a trailer in a run-down park, then a motel room with weekly rates, stayed with friends here and there between, and worked odd jobs sometimes.

Terry was a good-looking boy. He took after his father, who had only been in Queen's life a short time before liver cancer took him. She might have forgotten what the man looked like, except that Terry favored him so much. Queen knew that Wanda had waited for years for a proposal from Terry that would probably never happen. "Why buy the cow, when you get the milk for free?" Queen had said to Wanda once. Queen felt sorry for her in a way. Wanda had been bounced from one foster home to another during most of her childhood, after seeing her mother shot to death by her father. Every so often, Terry and Wanda would land on her front porch, asking for money and a place to stay. Queen had never said no.

"Well, did you get the job, Terry Dean?"

Terry slowly looked up at his mother and said, "The job. Yeah! Yeah, I got the job." He and Wanda weren't bothering with plates or utensils. They just stuffed a little of everything in their mouths as they went.

Queen folded her arms and leaned against the door jamb. "Well, what is it?

Terry stopped chewing and said, "What's what?

"The job, son! Where are you working?"

The egg carton slid out onto Terry's foot, breaking a couple of eggs. Yolks were oozing down the top of his shoe. He and Wanda burst out laughing again. Queen kept glaring until Terry caught his breath and said, "Yeah, I'm washing dishes at Sonny's Steakhouse."

"Well, congratulations." She handed Terry some paper towels to clean up the broken eggs. She knew she would have to go behind him and mop. "I reckon y'all will be wantin' to get your own place now. I hear there's one side of a nice duplex in Greenhurst available. You can afford it if Wanda'll get a job, too."

Terry's face fell grave. "First things first, Momma. I got to have transportation. So the first paycheck I get, I got to get me a car. I'll be walking until then." Queen knew he was asking to borrow her car to go to work. And there was no way she was giving in on that.

"Yep, reckon you'll be walkin'." With that, she disappeared into her work room, where Terry and Wanda were staying, to get some more thread.

A couple of weeks later, the pair were still residents of her work room. Their stuff was starting to spill out of the room and take over the house. A pair of shoes here, a knapsack there. They were getting more comfortable all the time. But Queen had stood firm on not lending her car and not giving rides. As Queen made a trip into town to deliver some work to Small Blessings, she passed Terry and Wanda walking up the road. She tooted her horn and waved, then hit the gas. *Give 'em an inch, and they'll take a mile,* she thought. A ride today would turn into a ride every day. Terry had finally flat-out asked to borrow the car, but Queen had told him she needed to use it.

That afternoon, Queen peered through the lace curtains when she heard an engine rumbling out front. A BMW with dark tinted windows and lots of chrome parked next to Queen's old Buick Skylark. When Wanda emerged from the passenger side, Queen smirked. "Mm-hm. Got somebody to give 'em a ride," she whispered to herself. But when Terry got out of the driver's door, Queen got a sinking feeling. She didn't want to know how he had gotten that car.

Terry grinned and waved at the car. "How do you like *this*, Momma?" He strutted up the front steps.

"You got this on dishwasher pay?" Queen wasn't smiling.

"What? No, Momma. I quit that job last week." Terry's face sank. "I got a better job now."

"Doin' *what*?!" Queen threw her hands up. Terry slouched as he glanced back at Wanda. She was standing next to the car with her arms folded and her jaw set. Queen took note of the fact that Wanda was wearing a new outfit. Something fancy from Belk's, she reckoned.

Terry moved closer up the stairs and lowered his voice a bit. "I'm in sales now."

Queen frowned and looked at her son sideways. "Sellin' what?"

"Well, you remember Walter?"

"Oh yeah, I know Walter. The one you call Scratch. He got you into this?"

Terry chuckled. "Yeah, but he don't go by Scratch when he's doin' business. He's all professional-like now. And I am, too. See, Scratch—uh, Walter said if you're gonna *be* successful, you gotta *look* successful. If you put a good image out there, people wanna do business with you 'cause they think other people already trust you."

"Ain't nobody but a fool gonna trust Scratch. And you still ain't told me what you're sellin'." Queen never liked Scratch because he was always in trouble, and she didn't want it to rub off on Terry. When they were teenagers, Scratch was the one who got caught making fake ID's. More recently, he had done hard time for practicing law without a license and embezzling hundreds of thousands of dollars.

"Well, Scratch, see, he gets things for people."

"What kind of things?"

"Well, cars, for one thing. Or heavy equipment, boats, four wheelers. He's kind of like a middle man. He calls it bein' a broker. Then he collects like a finder's fee. He's gotten real busy, see, and he needed me to come on with him and help. He hooks me up with the deal, and after I close it, I give him half and I keep half. He's got people he works with all over the east coast. I'm headed to Myrtle Beach next week to pick up a boat and haul it to North Carolina."

"This don't sound right. I don't like it."

"It's legit, I swear! Listen, some folks got to get rid of somethin' for one reason or another. You know, can't afford it no more . . ."

"Or it's hot . . ."

"What? No! Listen, Momma! We're *helping* people." Terry grinned and puffed his chest out. Then he pulled out the big roll of cash from his pocket and fanned it in front of his mother. "Look at *this,* Momma. I made it on my first day." Queen saw 10's and 100's flip past her nose.

"Well, you got wheels, and you got money. Now I reckon you got a place to stay, too. Glory, hallelujah, I can have my work room back. Lemme just help with gettin' your stuff together." She started into the front door.

"Well, not yet, Momma. We ain't found a place yet where we could move in right away. We're gonna be outta your hair soon enough, I promise, but we just need to stay here a couple more nights."

"Well, all right," Queen conceded. "But you're gonna take some of that big money you got there and order us some Chinese for supper."

A week later, Queen sat listening to another of her daughter's tirades on the phone. "Enough is enough, Momma! If you don't kick them out today, *I will.* I swear, I will come over there and throw their stuff out on the porch myself."

"They're goin' soon, Baby, I know they are. He said they signed a lease on a place yesterday. They just gotta get some furniture moved in there."

"A lease? Neither one of them got enough credit to borrow a stick of gum. Wonder what fool gonna let them rent?"

"Maybe they got no credit, but he's got money. I seen it. Big rolls of it. I don't know where he got it, but I'm sure that got 'em in. They go off during the day and they drive all over the place. They come in here late at night and just spend the night. They been to Myrtle Beach, Virginia Beach, I don't know where else. They're doin' *somethin'*."

"Yeah, *somethin'*," repeated Angel. "Somethin' illegal." Angel sighed. "I'm just concerned for you, Momma. You need to get em' out."

"Well, they said they had to drive to Florida today and wouldn't be back till late. I'll tell them in the mornin' to get their stuff out."

It was just after 2:00 a.m. when Queen heard something rumbling outside. She sat up and peeked out of the window next to her bed. Terry's car was backing down the side of the house. It stopped at the corner, under a tree. Two figures got out and tiptoed toward the back of the house. Queen lay down in her bed and listened for their footsteps and whispers, just to make double-sure it was Terry and Wanda. It was. She turned her face into her favorite down pillow and was asleep again within seconds.

The whole house shook and rattled. Queen sat up in bed, gasping. *Earthquake*, was her first thought. Then she realized it was someone banging on the front door and yelling. The clock said 2:35 a.m. Queen knew this had to be someone looking for her boy. The voice outside threatened to break in the door if no one would open it. Queen was fairly sure she heard "Dorchester County Sheriff" being shouted somewhere in the middle there. She pulled on her robe and stepped into her slippers. But as she rounded the corner to go open the front door, Terry gently pushed her back into her bedroom.

"Leave it alone, Momma," he whispered, his chin quivering and voice cracking. "Just go back to bed."

"What's goin' on, Terry Dean? This is *my* house! You tell me what's goin' on!" Queen demanded. She heard the screen on the back door tap shut. "They're at the back door, too?!" Terry shushed his mother repeatedly and told her that if they were quiet, the people would go away. But after a few minutes, someone at the back door was calling out that it was the Dorchester County Sheriff. Queen shuffled out of her room, with Terry pulling back on her, and realized the back door was already open. She waved the officers in. Terry took off out the front door, but there was an immediate scuffle. Rights were read loudly. Queen saw no fewer than four police cars, and blue lights were flashing through the dark night.

Queen took a ride in the back of a police car and answered a lot of questions, well into the morning. She thought the officers were very polite. They saw to her comfort, and she said their mothers should be proud to have such polite, professional sons. She didn't mind talking, and told all she knew about Terry and Wanda's new "business." She told all about how Scratch had gotten her son involved, and she was sure Scratch was the "boss" of the operation. Queen was incensed to find out that Wanda had not been arrested and was nowhere to be found at the scene. She remembered the back door being open, and the sound of the screen tapping the frame. She told the investigator she was sure Wanda had slipped out then. She was more than happy to give a detailed description of the woods behind her house, and all of the surrounding area.

Only a few minutes into the questioning, Queen heard commotion and recognized Angel's voice in the hallway. An officer opened the door, and Queen saw Angel being restrained as she hurled foul names through the air at her brother. He was in handcuffs, and leaned away from his sister, looking eager to get to the lock-up. As soon as the investigators were finished with Queen, Angel escorted her home and got her settled. The house had been upturned by policemen looking for drugs and stolen goods. Angel helped Queen put things back together.

Queen sat quietly humming to herself and smocking a baby boy's Jon Jon. She looked out the window every now and then. *Tomorrow,* she told herself, *I'll go into town.* She had several orders to take to Small Blessings. After a few minutes, she got up and went to the kitchen for some iced tea.

*The good Lord, He takes care of me,* she thought as she smiled. *Lordy, Lordy, please watch over my boy, Terry Dean, too.*

Terry sat on an armored bus, bound for a prison in Columbia. He stared out the window and wondered how long before he would be able to get parole. Maybe ten years, if he watched his back and didn't get into trouble. Scratch would probably be an old man before he got out. Repeat offender and all. The shoulder of the road sloped down into a swamp. A female hitchhiker stood on the side of the interstate with a small pack on her back. "Wanda," he said quietly, as they got closer. But then he shook his head. This woman had short, curly hair, and Wanda's was long. As the bus whizzed past her, the woman turned in time to lock eyes with Terry. Her mouth dropped open. Terry's did, too. "She changed her hair. She changed her hair," he said aloud. As he looked back, he saw a man in a red truck pulling over to give Wanda a ride. Terry's chest felt tight. Then he took a deep breath. *Wanda'll be all right,* he told himself.

Wanda was hungry, weary, and stone cold sober. She kept reaching to push back hair that wasn't there anymore. The curls had been a surprise, once the weight of her long hair was chopped off in the gas station bathroom. For the first time, since she had met Terry Dean Trapbear twenty years before, Wanda was alone and scared. She remembered Queen saying the good Lord watched over her. Wanda wondered if there was a good Lord who would watch over her, too.

When the red truck pulled over in front of her, Wanda was relieved and wary all at the same time. She climbed into the truck and thanked the driver for stopping. A Bible and a copy of American Hunter magazine lay on the bench seat next to him.

"Where are you headed?" he asked.

"Columbia," she answered. "The only family I got is on his way there now. He'll be expecting me."

# Thanks

I give thanks to God for daily inspiration, among other wonderful gifts too numerous to mention here. Next, this book would not have been possible without the patience and support of my husband and son while I spent hours, days, weeks, and months writing, revising and proofing. Thanks also to my supportive parents for their help and encouragement. Last, but not least, I must thank my friends (you know who you are!) for the encouragement. Keep it coming!